Sweet Sorrel Stand

By Yolanda T. Marshall

It was a hot day. The sun was shining, and the birds sang loudly from the black oak trees.

Rose and Nicolas were feeling thirsty after playing soccer in their backyard when their Mom called them inside for some cold water, before they would head to the Caribbean grocery store.

"Guess what would quench my thirst right now?" Rose asked.

"Lemonade?" replied Nicolas.

"No, something red and sweet," Rose said.

"Ah Ha! It must be your favourite drink!" Nicolas said. And they both yelled out at the same time, "Sorrel!"

They ran into the kitchen and asked their Mom to make a Sorrel drink.

"Please, Mommy, I know you usually only make it at Christmas time," Rose said, "but it will taste just as sweet with ice, on this hot, sunny day!"

Nicolas pleaded too, "And Mom, you said it is rich in Vitamin C, and it will keep us healthy!"

Their Mom couldn't resist; after all, they made valid reasons for wanting a Sorrel drink, and she loved it too.

"Hmm, I will make a big pot, but you will have to be patient and let it steep for a few hours," their Mom replied.

Rose and Nicolas admired the dried, red flowers.

"Dad said that this Sorrel plant is originally from West Africa," Nicolas said.

"That is correct, and it is a traditional drink for many Caribbean nations," their Mom replied, ".Sorrel drink is made with the roselle plant's flower, boiled with various spices and sugar."

"Roselle? Sounds like Rose's name," chimed in Nicolas. Rose smiled at her brother.

"Yes, hun, as sweet as your sister, Rose," their Mom replied.

Mom stirred the Sorrel drink in a huge, hot iron pot. The aroma spread through the house.

The children kept their eyes on the pot, as their mom dropped a large piece of orange peel into the boiling drink. The scent of the Sorrel heightened.

And their Mom asked, "Who wants to help me add the spices?"

"Me! Me!" they yelled excitedly.

Nicolas added cinnamon sticks and ginger. Rose added cloves and nutmeg. Their Mom stirred the Sorrel drink until all the ingredients mixed together. She conducted a little taste test with her wooden spoon. The children sipped a spoonful each and nodded in approval. They went to the grocery store, while the Sorrel drink cooled down.

When they returned, their Mom removed the sorrel petals and added brown sugar. They each enjoyed a tall glass of Sorrel drink with ice.

"Mom, we should make a Sorrel stand!" Rose proposed.

"WOW! We can sell each cup of cold Sorrel drink for one dollar," Nicolas said, "I bet we will make enough money to buy a new soccer ball."

Their Mom agreed, "You two are brilliant! I made enough Sorrel for your new business!"

Their Dad arrived home in time to set up the 'Sweet Sorrel Stand'. Nicolas and Rose wanted to share their favourite drink with their neighbours.

They called out to everyone who passed by, "Come get some cold Sorrel drink, sweet Sorrel on a sunny day!"

Their friends lined to buy a cup of Sorrel. Everyone loved it! This was the first taste of Sorrel for most who came to the stand.

"Now, this is really refreshing!"
said Mr. Shaw
"Oh my, you have a customer for life!"
promised Miss Myrtle.

Within hours, the word had spread, and the demand for Sorrel drink increased. Nicolas, Rose, and their parents made more Sorrel for the customers.

It was a successful day for the 'Sweet Sorrel Stand'!

Evening arrived, and it was time to close for the day.

"I am very proud of you two; you earned enough to afford a new soccer ball, to cover the expense of the ingredients, and to save in your piggy banks!" said their Dad.

Rose and Nicolas thanked their parents for all their help.

"Mom, maybe next time, we will make a coconut water stand!" Nicolas said.

"That's a *sweet* plan!" Rose agreed.

THE END

For my Parents, Herbert and Hazel Marshall

Published by Garnalma Press
www.Garnalma.com

ISBN: 978-0-9953103-7-7 (Hardcover Edition)
ISBN: 978-0-9953103-8-4 (Paperback Edition)

www.YTMarshall.com

CPSIA information can be obtained
at www.ICGtesting.com
Printed in the USA
LVHW070306140422
716183LV00001B/9